The Shadow Eater

The Shadow Eater

Matthew Petchinsky

The Shadow Eater: A Tale of Despair and Survival
By: Matthew Petchinsky

Chapter 1: The Vanishing

Hollow Creek was the kind of town where the biggest news might be the new paint job on the diner or the mayor's dog winning a local contest. It sat nestled in the crook of the Blackthorn Mountains, surrounded by dense, ancient forests that whispered with secrets carried on the wind. The residents liked it that way—quiet, predictable, and far removed from the chaos of the wider world.

But that predictability was shattered one crisp autumn evening when the sheriff's office received a frantic call.

"Sheriff Morgan, we've got a situation up at Blackthorn Trail," said Deputy Carla Hensley, her voice tight with tension as she leaned into the sheriff's office doorway.

Sheriff Caleb Morgan looked up from his cluttered desk, where he was halfway through a late-night sandwich. The sheriff was a bear of a man, with a graying beard and a disposition as steady as the mountains surrounding them. He chewed deliberately, his blue eyes narrowing. "What kind of situation?"

"Pete Morrison's boy, Tim, and his two friends never came home. They were supposed to be back by sundown." Carla hesitated, brushing a strand of auburn hair from her face. "Pete says they were camping out by Ironwood Clearing. The search party found their campsite... but not them."

Morgan set his sandwich down and stood, his six-foot-two frame seeming to fill the small room. "Alright. Let's head out. You got a flashlight? We'll need it. Blackthorn gets dark fast."

The drive to the trailhead was tense. Morgan kept his hands steady on the wheel, the old cruiser's headlights slicing through the encroaching darkness. Carla sat in the passenger seat, her fingers fidgeting with the flashlight in her lap.

"You think it's just kids being kids?" Carla ventured, though the nervous edge to her voice betrayed her doubt.

"Could be," Morgan replied gruffly. "Or it could be they got lost. Maybe twisted an ankle, wandered off the trail. Happens."

Carla nodded but said nothing. Hollow Creek was small, but its woods were vast and unforgiving. People didn't just wander off without leaving some kind of trace.

By the time they arrived, the search party had gathered at the edge of Ironwood Clearing. Pete Morrison, a wiry man with worry etched deep into his face, was pacing near the trail marker. A few others, flashlights in hand, milled about, their voices low and hushed.

"Morgan," Pete called out as soon as he spotted the sheriff. "It's bad. Real bad."

"Take a breath, Pete," Morgan said, clapping the man on the shoulder. "What's going on? Show me."

Pete led them up a narrow path into the clearing. The smell of burnt wood hit Morgan first, then the glow of a smoldering campfire came into view. Around it were three sleeping bags, perfectly unrolled. Nearby sat a small cooler and an open bag of marshmallows, some of them spilling out onto the ground. Nothing was disturbed—no signs of a struggle, no tracks leading away.

"It's like they just... vanished," Pete whispered, his voice trembling. "Tim wouldn't just leave his gear. None of them would."

Morgan crouched by the fire, holding a hand over the faint heat still radiating from the ashes. "This hasn't been out long. Maybe an hour or two." He stood and swept the beam of his flashlight across the area. "No signs of wildlife messing with the site. No blood, no footprints. Just... nothing."

"That's what I've been trying to tell you," Pete said, his voice rising. "It doesn't make sense!"

Morgan turned to Carla. "Get the dogs. If they wandered off, they couldn't have gone far."

"I'm on it," Carla said, pulling out her radio.

As she stepped away to make the call, Morgan walked the perimeter of the clearing. The woods were unnaturally silent, save for the crunch of leaves underfoot. He frowned, feeling a prickle of unease—a sensation he hadn't felt in years, not since his time as a rookie officer in the city.

He stopped abruptly, the beam of his flashlight catching something unusual at the base of a tree. Kneeling, he inspected it more closely: deep grooves etched into the bark, like claw marks. But they were too precise, too clean to be made by any animal he knew of.

"Sheriff?" Carla's voice called from behind him.

Morgan rose and turned, showing her the marks. "Seen anything like this before?"

Carla's eyes widened. "No. And I don't think I want to."

Before they could discuss it further, the sound of frantic barking echoed through the trees. The search dogs had arrived, their handlers struggling to keep up as the animals tugged at their leashes.

"Good. Let's see what they can find," Morgan said, waving the handlers forward.

The dogs sniffed around the campsite, circling the sleeping bags and cooler before suddenly stopping as one. They whimpered, tails tucked, and backed away, their bodies trembling.

"What the hell?" one of the handlers muttered, trying to coax his dog forward. "It's like they're scared of something."

Morgan's frown deepened. "Dogs don't spook this easy."

"It's not just the dogs," Carla said, her voice barely above a whisper. She pointed to the woods beyond the clearing. The darkness seemed... alive. Shadows shifted unnaturally, as if writhing just beyond the reach of their flashlights.

Morgan felt the hairs on the back of his neck rise. "Everyone back to the trailhead," he ordered, his tone leaving no room for argument.

By the time they returned to the cars, Pete was demanding answers. "What did you find? What's out there?"

Morgan held up a hand to calm him. "We don't know yet. But we'll keep looking. For now, I want everyone out of these woods."

"You're saying you're giving up?" Pete yelled, his face red with anger and fear.

"I'm saying we need daylight," Morgan said firmly. "We'll organize a larger search in the morning."

Pete looked like he wanted to argue, but Carla stepped in. "Pete, we're going to find them. But we need to do this right."

Reluctantly, Pete nodded, though his expression remained grim. The group dispersed, leaving Morgan and Carla standing by the cruiser.

"What do you think really happened, Sheriff?" Carla asked as they climbed in.

Morgan didn't answer immediately. He stared out at the darkened woods, a deep frown etched into his face. "I don't know. But whatever it is... it's not normal."

As they drove back to town, neither of them noticed the faint glow that flickered deep within the forest, like embers breathing to life. Something ancient had stirred in Hollow Creek—and it wasn't finished yet.

Chapter 2: Whispers in the Dark

The morning sun pierced through the heavy canopy of the Blackthorn Forest, casting long, dappled shadows on the forest floor. Despite the light, an oppressive stillness hung in the air, as if the trees themselves were holding their breath. A dozen search party members combed the area, their chatter low and their movements deliberate.

"Spread out but stay within shouting distance!" Sheriff Caleb Morgan called out, his voice carrying over the crunch of dead leaves. He stood at the edge of a ravine, scanning the dense foliage with a pair of binoculars. "If you find anything—anything at all—call it in."

"Got it, Sheriff," Deputy Carla Hensley replied, her tone as professional as she could manage despite the pit in her stomach. She adjusted her flashlight and glanced nervously at the shadows. Even in the daylight, they seemed darker than they should have been, deeper, almost alive.

"Sheriff!" a voice yelled from the eastern edge of the search grid. "We've got something!"

Morgan jogged toward the call, his boots crunching on brittle branches. When he arrived, he found Hank Waller, one of the volunteer searchers, standing near a cluster of trees. His face was pale, and his hands trembled as he pointed to the ground.

"What is it, Hank?" Morgan asked, stepping closer.

Hank swallowed hard and pointed again. "Look."

At the base of a tree, the earth was gouged deeply, as if by massive claws. Surrounding it were more of the strange, clean-edged markings like the ones Morgan had seen the night before. They formed a loose circle, and in the center lay a patch of ash-blackened grass. It smelled faintly of sulfur.

"Jesus," Carla muttered, arriving behind them. "What could do that?"

Morgan didn't answer immediately. He crouched, running his fingers over one of the grooves in the bark. It was ice-cold to the touch. He drew his hand back quickly, a faint tingling sensation lingering on his fingertips.

"We'll flag this area," Morgan said, standing abruptly. "Keep moving, but stay alert. I don't like this."

The day dragged on with little progress. As dusk fell, the search party returned to the trailhead, empty-handed and deflated. Pete Morrison was there, his eyes bloodshot from lack of sleep.

"You're telling me you found *nothing*?" he demanded, his voice hoarse. "Not even a goddamn footprint?"

Morgan shook his head. "We're doing everything we can, Pete."

"It's not enough!" Pete roared, his grief boiling over. "My boy is out there, Sheriff, and you're telling me you don't have a clue where to even look?"

"Pete—" Carla began, but Pete cut her off.

"No! Don't you 'Pete' me! You're all out here playing search-and-rescue while my son—" His voice broke, and he turned away, shaking his head.

Morgan watched him go, his chest tightening with guilt. He exchanged a glance with Carla, who looked equally troubled.

"What now?" she asked quietly.

"We keep looking," Morgan said. "But I need to start asking questions. Something about this feels... wrong."

That evening, Morgan stopped by the Hollow Creek Diner. It was the unofficial hub of local gossip, and he figured if anyone had seen or heard anything strange, word would have reached the regulars by now.

The bell above the door jingled as he entered. A few heads turned, and the low murmur of conversation briefly quieted before resuming. Morgan took a seat at the counter, nodding to Mary Lou, the elderly waitress who'd been slinging coffee since before he was born.

"Evening, Sheriff," she said, pouring him a steaming cup without asking. "Rough day?"

"You could say that," he replied, cradling the mug in his hands. "You hear anything about those missing kids?"

Mary Lou's cheerful expression faltered. She glanced around, then leaned in closer. "You mean besides half the town thinking it's some kind of animal?"

"Yeah, besides that."

She hesitated, her voice dropping to a whisper. "There's talk about something... unnatural. Some of the old-timers are saying it's the Shadow Eater."

Morgan raised an eyebrow. "The what?"

"The Shadow Eater," a gravelly voice interjected. Morgan turned to see Joe Wilkes, a retired logger, sitting a few stools down. He sipped his coffee, his rheumy eyes gleaming with grim certainty. "You've never heard of it? Thought everyone around here knew that story."

"Enlighten me," Morgan said, setting his mug down.

Joe leaned forward, his voice low but steady. "It's an old legend. Goes back to the earliest settlers. They said something lived in these woods—something that wasn't supposed to. It fed on light, life, anything it could get its claws on. Called it the Shadow Eater."

"Sounds like a campfire story," Morgan said, though his tone lacked conviction.

Joe's gaze hardened. "You think I'm joking? You ask anyone who's been in these woods long enough. They'll tell you about the cold spots, the shadows that move when they shouldn't, the noises..."

"What kind of noises?" Carla, who had just walked in, asked as she slid onto the stool next to Morgan.

Joe glanced at her. "A growl, low and deep. Not like any animal you've ever heard. And if you hear it, you'd best pray you don't see what comes next."

"Let me guess," Morgan said dryly. "The monster comes out, eats people, and vanishes back into the shadows."

Joe shook his head. "Not just people. It'll eat anything. Light, warmth, even the will to fight. That's why folks don't survive seeing it. They don't have the strength to run."

Mary Lou crossed herself, muttering a quiet prayer. Carla shot Morgan a nervous glance.

"Have you seen it?" Morgan asked Joe directly.

Joe hesitated, then nodded. "Once. Years ago, when I was out logging near Ironwood Clearing. Saw something dark moving through the trees, but it wasn't casting a shadow—it *was* the shadow. Everything around it froze. Not just the air—time itself felt wrong."

"What did you do?" Carla asked, her voice barely above a whisper.

Joe's lips pressed into a thin line. "Ran like hell. Didn't stop till I was back in town."

Later, as Morgan and Carla left the diner, she spoke up. "You don't really believe that, do you?"

"I don't know what to believe anymore," Morgan admitted. "But whatever's out there, it's scaring the hell out of people. And if we don't figure it out soon, it's going to get worse."

As they walked to the cruiser, a cold wind swept through the street, sending a shiver down both their spines. Morgan glanced back toward the forest, where the shadows seemed to stretch and shift under the pale glow of the streetlights.

Somewhere deep in the woods, something was watching—and waiting.

Chapter 3: The First Blood

The early morning mist clung to the trees like a shroud as Sheriff Caleb Morgan pulled his cruiser to the side of the dirt road leading to Blackthorn Trail. The call had come in just before dawn: a body had been found hanging from a tree near the old logging camp. The voice on the other end of the line—Tom Jenkins, another local hunter—had been shaking with fear.

Morgan stepped out of the car, adjusting his hat against the biting chill. He spotted Jenkins pacing near the edge of the woods, his rifle slung over one shoulder.

"Tom," Morgan called as he approached. "What's this about a body?"

Jenkins turned sharply, his eyes wide with fear. "Sheriff... it's bad. Real bad."

"Show me," Morgan said, his voice steady, though a knot was already forming in his stomach.

The two men trudged through the forest, the damp ground muffling their footsteps. As they approached the clearing, Morgan noticed an unnatural stillness in the air. Even the birds seemed to have fallen silent.

"There," Jenkins whispered, pointing a trembling finger ahead.

Morgan followed his gaze and felt his stomach churn. Hanging from a thick branch was the lifeless body of Hank Keller, a seasoned hunter who had called Hollow Creek home for decades. His torso was shredded, the wounds deep and jagged, exposing bone in places. Blood dripped steadily from his body, pooling on the ground below.

Morgan stepped closer, his boots crunching on fallen leaves. "Stay back, Tom."

He scanned the area, looking for any signs of an animal. The ground beneath the body was undisturbed, with no tracks leading in or out. It was as if Hank had been dropped from the sky and hung there like a grotesque marionette.

"What kind of animal could do this?" Jenkins asked, his voice shaking.

Morgan didn't answer. Instead, he focused on the tree itself. Strange claw marks—similar to those he'd seen near the teens' campsite—were scorched into the bark. They formed a circular pattern around the branch where Hank's body hung, as though the tree itself had been marked by whatever had killed him.

Deputy Carla Hensley arrived minutes later, her face pale as she took in the scene. "Oh my God. Sheriff, this is…" She trailed off, struggling to find the words.

"Get the crime scene kit from the car," Morgan said tersely. "And radio the coroner. Tell him we've got a priority one."

Carla nodded, quickly retreating to the cruiser. Jenkins, still standing a few feet away, crossed himself. "I told you, Sheriff. There's something out here."

"I don't need ghost stories right now, Tom," Morgan snapped. "Go back to town. We'll handle this."

Jenkins hesitated but eventually nodded, disappearing down the trail. Morgan turned back to the body, his jaw tightening. He had seen a lot during his time as a city cop before returning to Hollow Creek, but this… this was unlike anything he had encountered.

An hour later, the crime scene was bustling with activity. The coroner, Dr. Amelia Briggs, was crouched near the body, her gloved hands carefully inspecting the wounds. Carla stood nearby, snapping photos and jotting down notes.

"What do you think, Doc?" Morgan asked, standing over her.

Dr. Briggs shook her head. "I don't know what to tell you, Sheriff. These wounds… they're not consistent with any animal attack I've ever seen. Too deep for a bear, too irregular for a big cat. And these markings on the tree—" She gestured to the scorched claw marks. "—I've got no explanation for those."

Morgan frowned. "Could it be some kind of hoax? Someone trying to stir up fear?"

Briggs looked up at him, her expression grim. "If this is a hoax, it's the most elaborate one I've ever seen. And those wounds are real. Whatever did this was big and powerful."

Carla spoke up, her voice uneasy. "Sheriff, we should talk about the elephant in the room."

Morgan sighed. "You mean the Shadow Eater?"

Carla nodded. "The whole town's been buzzing about it ever since the teens disappeared. And now this? People are going to lose their minds."

"I'm not feeding into that hysteria," Morgan said firmly. "Legends don't kill people. Something real did this, and we're going to find out what."

By the afternoon, the body had been taken to the morgue, and the sheriff's office was buzzing with speculation. Morgan called a town meeting at the community center, hoping to get ahead of the rumors spreading like wildfire.

The room was packed, the air thick with unease. Pete Morrison sat near the front, his face a mask of grief and anger. Jenkins stood in the back, his rifle still slung over his shoulder.

Morgan stepped onto the small stage and raised his hands for silence. "I know everyone's scared," he began, his voice steady. "And I know you've all heard the stories. But I'm here to tell you, there's no monster in these woods. We've got an animal attack, plain and simple. I need everyone to stay calm and let us do our job."

"That wasn't an animal!" Jenkins shouted from the back. "I saw those marks! I saw the body! That thing ain't natural!"

Murmurs of agreement rippled through the crowd. Morgan gritted his teeth. "I'm not saying it's not dangerous," he said. "But spreading fear isn't going to help. Stay out of the woods, lock your doors, and let my team handle this."

"What about my son?" Pete Morrison demanded, rising to his feet. "You promised you'd find him, Sheriff. Instead, we've got another body."

Morgan met Pete's gaze. "We're not giving up, Pete. I swear to you, we'll find your boy."

Pete's face twisted with anger and pain, but he said nothing more. He sat back down, his hands clenched into fists.

Later that evening, Morgan sat alone in his office, staring at the crime scene photos spread out on his desk. The claw marks on the tree, the strange wounds, the lack of any tracks or signs of struggle—it all pointed to something he couldn't explain.

A knock at the door pulled him from his thoughts. Carla stepped in, a file in her hands. "Forensics report," she said, setting it on his desk.

Morgan opened it and scanned the contents. His brow furrowed. "The wounds... they're burned?"

Carla nodded. "Dr. Briggs says it's like the tissue was cauterized as it was torn. Whatever did this wasn't just big—it was hot."

Morgan leaned back in his chair, the weight of the situation settling on his shoulders. "What the hell are we dealing with, Carla?"

"I don't know, Sheriff," she said quietly. "But whatever it is, it's not done."

Morgan looked out the window, where the dark silhouette of the Blackthorn Forest loomed against the fading light. For the first time, he felt a flicker of doubt—a small, gnawing voice in the back of his mind whispering that maybe, just maybe, the legends were true.

Chapter 4: Lockdown

The tension in Hollow Creek was palpable as the sun set behind the Blackthorn Mountains, casting long shadows that seemed to creep and stretch unnaturally across the town. Sheriff Caleb Morgan stood in the mayor's office, his hat clutched in his hands as he listened to Mayor Evelyn Grayson pace back and forth, her high heels clicking sharply against the hardwood floor.

"Sheriff, this town is on the verge of losing it," Evelyn said, her tone clipped but laced with unease. Her usually immaculate blonde hair was slightly disheveled, and dark circles under her eyes hinted at sleepless nights. "We've had two town meetings in as many days, and the rumors are spreading faster than we can contain them. We need to act."

"I agree," Morgan said, his voice steady. "But locking people in their homes won't stop whatever's out there. We don't even know what we're dealing with yet."

Evelyn stopped pacing and turned to him, her eyes narrowing. "So what do you suggest? Let everyone carry on as if there isn't a... a monster out there?"

Morgan's jaw tightened. "I'm saying we focus on protecting the people who are vulnerable. Increase patrols, set up safe zones—"

Evelyn cut him off, her voice rising. "No, Caleb. We're imposing a curfew. Starting tonight. I've already drafted the order. No one outside after sunset. This isn't up for debate."

Morgan sighed, resisting the urge to argue further. He could see the fear in Evelyn's eyes, and he knew she wasn't entirely wrong. "Fine. But if we're doing this, I need more deputies. We're stretched thin as it is."

"You'll get them," Evelyn promised. "I'll call in reinforcements from Ridgeway County. But, Caleb—" She hesitated, her voice softening. "You need to find out what's going on before more people die."

The curfew was announced that afternoon, sending a ripple of anxiety through the town. As Morgan and Deputy Carla Hensley patrolled the streets, they encountered a mix of reactions—some residents were visibly relieved, while others were defiant.

"This is ridiculous," grumbled Ed Thomas, the owner of the local hardware store, as he locked up for the night. "You think some boogeyman's gonna stop me from running my business?"

"Ed," Morgan said patiently, "this is for your safety. Just get home, lock your doors, and stay inside."

Ed muttered something under his breath but complied, shuffling off toward his truck. Carla watched him go, her expression troubled.

"Do you really think this curfew will make a difference?" she asked as they got back into the cruiser.

Morgan glanced at her, his face grim. "I don't know. But it's better than doing nothing."

The streets of Hollow Creek were eerily silent as night fell. Lights flickered on in the houses, and curtains were drawn tight. Patrol cars cruised slowly through the neighborhoods, their spotlights sweeping across empty yards and shadowed alleyways.

Around midnight, Morgan was parked outside the elementary school when his radio crackled to life. "Sheriff, we've got a report of something... strange on Maple Avenue," Carla's voice said, laced with tension.

"What kind of strange?" Morgan asked, already shifting the car into gear.

"Woman says she saw a... shadow moving in her yard. But there wasn't anything casting it."

Morgan's grip tightened on the steering wheel. "I'm on my way."

When Morgan arrived at the house, he found Carla standing on the front porch with an elderly woman wrapped in a shawl. The woman's hands were shaking as she clutched a cup of tea.

"Mrs. Wilkins, this is Sheriff Morgan," Carla said gently.

Morgan tipped his hat. "Ma'am. Can you tell me what you saw?"

Mrs. Wilkins nodded shakily. "It was out there," she said, pointing toward the backyard. "I saw it through the window—something moving, but it wasn't a person. It was... black, like smoke. And the air got so cold..."

Morgan exchanged a glance with Carla. "Did you hear anything?"

"A low growl," Mrs. Wilkins whispered. "Deep and... unnatural."

"Stay inside," Morgan said firmly. "Lock your doors and windows. We'll take a look."

Carla followed him into the backyard, their flashlights cutting through the darkness. The beam of Morgan's light fell on the frost-covered grass, and he crouched to inspect it. The temperature had dropped sharply, the air biting against their skin.

"Over here," Carla whispered, her light catching something on the ground.

Morgan approached and saw claw marks gouged into the bark of a tree, similar to the ones they'd found at the previous crime scenes. But this time, they were accompanied by something else—long, jagged scratches in the dirt, as though something massive had been dragged across the yard.

Before they could investigate further, a blood-curdling scream pierced the night, coming from a few streets over.

The two deputies sprinted back to their car and raced toward the source of the scream. They arrived at a modest two-story house, its front door ajar. Inside, the air was suffocatingly cold, and an unnatural darkness seemed to cling to the walls.

Morgan drew his weapon, signaling for Carla to follow. "Stay close."

They moved through the house, their flashlights barely cutting through the oppressive blackness. In the living room, they found the bodies—a family of four, their faces frozen in expressions of pure terror. Blood pooled around them, the floor slick with it. The walls were marked with deep gouges, and the furniture was overturned.

"What the hell happened here?" Carla whispered, her voice trembling.

Morgan's flashlight flickered, the beam sputtering as if something was interfering with it. He froze, his breath visible in the frigid air. A low, guttural growl echoed through the room.

"Sheriff..." Carla said, her voice barely audible.

A shadow moved in the corner of Morgan's vision, sliding along the wall like liquid. It coalesced into a vague, humanoid shape, its eyes glowing faintly red. The growl deepened, resonating through the room.

"Get back!" Morgan shouted, firing his weapon.

The bullets passed through the shadow, striking the wall behind it. The entity let out an ear-splitting screech, the sound vibrating in their bones. It lunged toward them, and Morgan grabbed Carla, pulling her toward the door.

"Move!" he barked.

They stumbled out onto the lawn, slamming the door behind them. The house fell silent, the unnatural cold dissipating. Morgan turned to Carla, his chest heaving.

"Did you see that?" she asked, her face pale.

"Yeah," Morgan said, his voice grim. "I saw it."

By morning, news of the attack had spread through the town. The mayor called an emergency meeting, her face pale as she addressed the gathered residents.

"We're dealing with something unprecedented," she said. "But I promise you, we will figure out how to stop it. Until then, the curfew remains in effect. Do not leave your homes at night."

Morgan stood at the back of the room, his arms crossed. He knew the curfew wouldn't stop the Shadow Eater. Whatever this thing was, it wasn't bound by doors or walls. And it wasn't done with Hollow Creek.

Chapter 5: The Scholar's Warning

The morning was gray and overcast as Sheriff Caleb Morgan pulled into the Hollow Creek library's parking lot. It wasn't often he found himself here, but the mayor had insisted on bringing in an expert to shed some light on the situation. He wasn't thrilled about it, but after what he and Deputy Carla Hensley had seen the night before, he wasn't about to dismiss any help.

Inside, the library smelled of old paper and varnished wood. Seated at a long table near the reference section was Dr. Emily Carson, a petite woman in her mid-40s with sharp green eyes behind wire-rimmed glasses. Her auburn hair was tied in a loose bun, and the table before her was piled with books, maps, and a laptop.

"Sheriff Morgan," she greeted, standing to shake his hand. "Thank you for meeting with me."

"Dr. Carson," Morgan replied, his handshake firm. "The mayor said you might have some answers. I'm all ears."

"Let's hope I do," Emily said, gesturing for him to sit. "I've been reviewing accounts of strange disappearances and deaths in this area over the past two centuries. What I've found is... troubling."

"Troubling how?" Morgan asked, taking a seat across from her.

Emily slid a worn leather-bound book toward him. "Have you heard of the 'Shadow Eater'?"

Morgan's jaw tightened. The term had been floating around town ever since the first disappearance. "A few times. Mostly from old-timers. What is it?"

"It's not just a local legend," Emily began, flipping open the book to a page filled with hand-drawn illustrations. One depicted a swirling mass of shadow with glowing red eyes. "Stories of a shadow-like entity have been recorded in folklore around the world. Different cultures call it by different names, but the descriptions are eerily similar: a creature that moves like living darkness, consuming light, warmth, and life it-self."

Morgan frowned, leaning closer to the book. "So what are we talking about here? Some kind of ghost?"

"No," Emily said firmly. "It's much worse. The Shadow Eater isn't a spirit or a demon—it's something older, something primordial. It's been described as a force of entropy, a creature born of the void before creation."

Morgan leaned back, his skepticism returning. "You expect me to believe we're dealing with some ancient boogeyman?"

Emily met his gaze, her green eyes steady. "Sheriff, I don't expect you to believe anything yet. But tell me—what have you seen? What happened at that house last night?"

Morgan hesitated. He hadn't spoken to anyone about the shadowy figure he and Carla had encountered. But something about Emily's calm demeanor made him want to open up.

"We saw something," he admitted. "It wasn't human. It wasn't... anything I've ever seen before. It moved like smoke but felt solid. And the air—" He shook his head. "It was so cold, like it was draining the heat right out of the room."

Emily nodded, as though she'd expected his answer. "That's exactly what it does. The Shadow Eater consumes not just physical light and heat but also the life force of its victims. It leaves behind nothing but fear and death."

At that moment, Deputy Carla Hensley entered the library, a thermos of coffee in hand. "Sheriff," she said, nodding to Emily. "Sorry to interrupt, but we've got another incident report—someone spotted more claw marks near the high school."

Morgan stood, slipping his hat back on. "Let's go."

"Wait," Emily said, rising as well. "I need to see this. The patterns of the claw marks might tell us something."

Morgan raised an eyebrow. "You sure about that, Doc? It's not exactly safe out there."

"I'm not afraid," Emily said simply. "If I'm going to help you, I need to see everything firsthand."

The three of them drove to the high school in silence, the tension palpable. When they arrived, they found a group of teachers and students gathered near the athletic field, their faces pale as they stared at the ground.

"Step back, folks," Morgan called, his authoritative tone scattering the onlookers. "Let us through."

At the center of the commotion was another patch of scorched earth, surrounded by deep claw marks gouged into the grass and dirt. Emily knelt to examine the marks, her brow furrowed.

"Definitely not an animal," she murmured. "These grooves are too uniform, too deliberate."

Carla crouched beside her. "So what are they? Footprints?"

Emily shook her head. "Not quite. They're more like... anchors. The creature uses them to stabilize itself when it manifests in our plane."

Morgan crossed his arms, his frustration mounting. "You keep talking about this thing like it's some kind of interdimensional monster. How do we fight it?"

Emily stood, brushing dirt from her hands. "That's the problem, Sheriff. You can't fight it—not in the traditional sense."

"What the hell does that mean?" Carla asked, her voice rising. "Are you saying we're just supposed to sit here and let it pick us off?"

"No," Emily said, her tone firm. "But the Shadow Eater can't be killed like an animal or a person. It's a being of pure entropy. The only way to stop it is to disrupt its feeding cycle."

"And how do we do that?" Morgan asked, his skepticism giving way to desperation.

Emily hesitated, then said, "There are rituals. Ancient ones. They're not easy, and they come with risks, but they might be our best chance."

"Rituals?" Morgan repeated, his voice flat. "You're telling me the only way to stop this thing is with magic?"

"Call it what you want," Emily replied. "But the people who've survived encounters with the Shadow Eater all used these methods. The problem is, the rituals require a very specific set of conditions—and a sacrifice."

Carla stared at her. "A sacrifice? What kind of sacrifice?"

"Usually... life," Emily said reluctantly. "Someone has to willingly offer their energy to weaken the creature."

Morgan's face darkened. "I'm not sacrificing anyone. There's got to be another way."

Emily sighed. "I'm not saying it's the only way, but it's the most reliable. And if we don't act soon, the Shadow Eater will only grow stronger. It's feeding off this town's fear, its despair. The more it consumes, the harder it will be to stop."

As they left the high school, Morgan's mind raced. He didn't believe in monsters, not really, but after everything he'd seen—and everything Emily had told him—he couldn't deny that something unnatural was at work in Hollow Creek.

Carla broke the silence as they got back into the cruiser. "Do you trust her?"

"I don't know," Morgan admitted. "But if she's right, we're going to need all the help we can get."

Emily, seated in the back, leaned forward. "Sheriff, I know this is hard to accept. But you need to understand—this thing isn't going to stop on its own. If we don't find a way to stop it, it'll destroy everything."

Morgan nodded grimly, his grip tightening on the steering wheel. "Then we'd better figure this out fast."

In the distance, the Blackthorn Forest loomed, its shadows darker than ever, as though the trees themselves were harboring something ancient and hungry.

Chapter 6: The Mass Exodus

Hollow Creek's small-town charm had always been its pride. Neighbors trusted one another, doors were rarely locked, and even the busiest streets were little more than quiet lanes flanked by maple and oak trees. But now, the streets were gridlocked with cars, trucks, and U-Hauls as terrified residents packed their belongings and fled.

Sheriff Caleb Morgan stood on the steps of Town Hall, his hands on his hips, surveying the chaos unfolding below. People shouted over one another as they loaded vehicles, their voices panicked and shrill. A young woman clutched her crying toddler while her husband argued with an elderly man over a gas pump. The atmosphere was thick with fear.

"Sheriff!" Carla Hensley jogged up to him, her face flushed. "It's getting worse. The gas station's out of fuel, and the grocery store's practically empty. People are starting to fight over supplies."

Morgan rubbed his temples. "What did you expect? Half the town's trying to leave all at once."

"I don't think it's just here," Carla added, lowering her voice. "I just got off the radio with the state patrol. They're reporting abandoned vehicles on Route 17—dozens of them. Drivers missing, no sign of where they went."

Morgan's head snapped up. "Abandoned? Missing how?"

"Just... gone," Carla said, her tone grim. "Some of the cars were still running when they were found. Whatever's happening here, it's spreading."

Morgan and Carla stepped into the Town Hall, where Mayor Evelyn Grayson was pacing in her office, her cellphone glued to her ear. She slammed it down as soon as she saw them.

"Caleb," she said, her voice tight, "we've got a situation."

"No kidding," Morgan replied. "Half the town's trying to get out of here."

"It's not just Hollow Creek anymore," Evelyn said, gesturing to her laptop. The screen displayed a news broadcast from a nearby city, where a frantic reporter stood in front of flashing police lights.

"...authorities have no explanation for the sudden disappearance of over twenty commuters on Highway 9," the reporter said. "Witnesses describe seeing strange shadows on the road before the victims vanished. Police are urging residents to stay indoors..."

Morgan exchanged a look with Carla. "This thing's spreading faster than we thought."

Evelyn sank into her chair, burying her face in her hands. "If we don't get a handle on this, there won't be a town left to save."

That evening, as the exodus continued, Morgan and Carla patrolled the outskirts of town. The roads were clogged with cars, their headlights cutting through the growing darkness. Families huddled inside vehicles, their faces pale and drawn.

"Sheriff," Carla said, pointing to the shoulder of the road. "Over there."

Morgan pulled the cruiser to a stop and stepped out. A sedan sat abandoned, its driver's door hanging open. The headlights illuminated the surrounding trees, but there was no sign of the driver or passengers. The car's engine was still running.

"What the hell..." Morgan muttered, drawing his flashlight.

He shone the beam into the forest, scanning the underbrush. The air was heavy and cold, and the familiar sound of insects and rustling leaves was conspicuously absent.

"Sheriff, over here!" Carla called, crouching near the car.

Morgan joined her, his stomach sinking as he saw the footprints. They led from the car into the woods but ended abruptly, as though the person had simply vanished.

"Another one," Carla said, her voice barely above a whisper.

Morgan straightened, his jaw tight. "Get the license plate. We'll need to report this one."

As they returned to the cruiser, Morgan caught movement out of the corner of his eye. A shadow—too large and fluid to be human—slid between the trees. He froze, gripping Carla's arm.

"Did you see that?" he whispered.

Carla nodded, her hand hovering over her holstered weapon. "Yeah."

"Let's go," Morgan said, his voice low. "We're sitting ducks out here."

By the time they returned to town, the streets were nearly empty. Most of the residents had fled, leaving behind shuttered homes and darkened storefronts. Morgan parked outside the sheriff's office, and the two of them sat in silence for a moment.

"What do we do now?" Carla asked, her voice heavy with exhaustion.

Morgan stared out the window, his mind racing. "We call for backup. State police, National Guard—hell, anyone who'll listen. If this thing's spreading, we're going to need all the help we can get."

"And if they don't believe us?"

Morgan turned to her, his expression grim. "Then we deal with it ourselves."

The next morning, Dr. Emily Carson arrived at the sheriff's office, her arms laden with books and maps. "I've been researching similar events in other parts of the world," she said, setting her materials on Morgan's desk. "And I think I've found a pattern."

"Pattern?" Morgan asked, leaning forward.

Emily spread out a map of the region, marking several points with a pen. "These incidents—mass disappearances, strange shadows, unexplained cold spots—they've all happened in isolated areas, always near dense forests or mountains."

"Like Hollow Creek," Carla said, peering over Morgan's shoulder.

"Exactly," Emily said. "And in every case, the phenomenon spreads outward, consuming nearby towns and cities. It doesn't stop until there's nothing left to feed on."

Morgan rubbed his chin, his frustration mounting. "So you're saying this thing is going to wipe out the whole region?"

"Not if we can stop it," Emily said firmly. "But we have to act quickly. The longer it's allowed to feed, the stronger it becomes."

"And how do we stop it?" Carla asked. "You mentioned rituals before."

Emily hesitated. "The rituals might slow it down, but to truly banish it, we'll need something stronger—something that can sever its connection to this plane entirely."

"And what's that?" Morgan pressed.

Emily met his gaze. "A sacrifice. Someone willing to offer themselves as a conduit to draw the creature back into the void."

Carla's face paled. "You can't be serious."

"I don't like it any more than you do," Emily said. "But this isn't just about Hollow Creek anymore. If we don't stop it here, it'll spread across the entire state—maybe even the country."

Morgan sat back, the weight of the situation pressing down on him. "We'll need a plan," he said finally. "Something to buy us time while we figure out the details."

Emily nodded. "Agreed. But whatever we do, we need to move fast. The Shadow Eater won't wait."

Outside, the wind howled through the empty streets, carrying with it an unnatural chill. Hollow Creek was on the brink of collapse, and the battle for its survival was just beginning.

Chapter 7: The Chilling Broadcast

The hum of fluorescent lights buzzed overhead in the Hollow Creek sheriff's office as Sheriff Caleb Morgan sat at his desk, his face illuminated by the glow of his computer screen. Deputy Carla Hensley stood beside him, arms crossed, staring at the screen with a deep frown.

"You have to see this," she said, gesturing toward the screen. "It's all over the internet."

Morgan clicked the link she'd sent him, opening a video titled, *"The Shadow Is Real—Live Footage from Hollow Creek."* It had been uploaded less than six hours ago and already had over two million views. The thumbnail showed a young man, his face pale and drenched in sweat, holding a flashlight under his chin in a dark room.

"Who is this guy?" Morgan asked.

"Name's Mark Hayes," Carla replied. "He's not from Hollow Creek—lives about twenty miles out in Ridgeway. His video started going viral around midnight. People are calling it a hoax, but... just watch."

Morgan hit play.

The video opened with static before Mark's panicked face filled the screen. His hair was disheveled, and his voice trembled as he spoke.

"Okay, uh... this is Mark Hayes. I don't know if anyone's gonna see this, but I need to document what's happening." He glanced over his shoulder, his flashlight beam sweeping across the unfinished basement walls. "Something's in my house."

The camera shook as he panned it around the room. Shadows danced across the cinderblock walls, but nothing out of the ordinary appeared. Mark's breathing was labored, and he muttered to himself, his words barely audible.

"It started a couple of hours ago," he continued. "Lights flickering, weird noises. I thought it was just a power surge or maybe a raccoon in the attic, but then... then I saw it."

The flashlight beam trembled as Mark aimed it at the far corner of the basement. "I swear, it was right there. This... this shadow. It wasn't just dark—it *moved*. Like it was alive."

The screen flickered, static briefly distorting the image before snapping back to Mark's terrified face. "It's still here. I can feel it. The air's so cold I can see my breath. I don't know what to do."

Mark's voice cracked, and the camera whipped around as a low growl echoed through the basement. It was deep and guttural, almost inhuman. Mark screamed, dropping the flashlight. The screen went black, but the audio continued.

"It's here! Oh God, it's here!" Mark shouted, his voice rising in pitch.

The growl grew louder, almost deafening, before the sound abruptly cut off. For a moment, there was only silence, and then a single, faint whisper: "Light... fades..."

The video ended with a burst of static.

Morgan leaned back in his chair, his face grim. "Jesus Christ."

Carla crossed her arms tighter. "It's not just the video, Sheriff. People are losing their minds over this. The comment section is a war zone—half of them think it's fake, the other half are convinced it's the apocalypse."

"What about Mark?" Morgan asked. "Anyone check on him?"

Carla shook her head. "I called Ridgeway PD. They sent someone to his house, but when they got there, it was empty. No sign of Mark, no signs of a struggle. Just... gone."

Morgan rubbed his temples, the weight of the situation pressing down on him. "This is exactly what we don't need right now. The whole town's already on edge, and now this thing's going viral."

"It's not just the town anymore," Carla said. "It's spreading. People all over the state are talking about it. Hashtags, conspiracy forums, even mainstream news sites are picking it up."

"Damn it," Morgan muttered. "The last thing we need is national attention. That'll bring reporters, thrill-seekers, and God knows what else."

A knock at the office door interrupted them. Dr. Emily Carson stepped inside, her arms full of books and papers. "I saw the video," she said without preamble. "It's worse than I thought."

Morgan gestured for her to sit. "What do you mean?"

Emily set down her materials and opened a leather-bound journal, flipping to a page filled with handwritten notes. "The Shadow Eater thrives on fear," she explained. "It's not just a predator—it's a psychological parasite. The more people believe in it, the stronger it becomes."

"So this video..." Carla began.

"Is like pouring gasoline on a fire," Emily finished. "Millions of people are watching it, talking about it, fearing it. That fear feeds the entity, gives it more power, more reach."

Morgan swore under his breath. "Can we take it down? Stop it from spreading?"

"It's already too late," Emily said. "Even if you delete the video, the damage is done. People have seen it, shared it. The fear is out there now."

Carla frowned. "So what do we do?"

"We have to contain the fear," Emily said. "If people believe the video is fake, it might weaken the Shadow Eater's hold."

Morgan looked skeptical. "And how do we do that? Issue a statement saying it's a hoax?"

"It's a start," Emily said. "But it won't be enough. We need a distraction—something to shift the narrative away from the Shadow Eater."

Later that day, the mayor held a press conference. Standing at a podium outside Town Hall, Evelyn Grayson addressed a crowd of reporters and concerned citizens. Morgan and Carla stood behind her, their expressions stoic.

"I want to assure everyone," Evelyn began, "that the video circulating online is nothing more than a hoax. While we take reports of unusual activity seriously, there is no evidence to support the existence of any so-called 'Shadow Eater.'"

The reporters erupted with questions, their voices overlapping. "Mayor Grayson, what about the missing people? What's being done to investigate their disappearances?"

Evelyn raised her hands for silence. "We are working closely with law enforcement to investigate every report. Our priority is the safety and well-being of our residents."

As the press conference continued, Morgan leaned toward Carla. "Think they'll buy it?"

Carla shook her head. "Not a chance."

That night, as Hollow Creek fell into uneasy silence, Morgan sat alone in his office, replaying the video on his computer. No matter how many times he watched it, the ending sent a chill down his spine.

The growl, the scream, the whisper—it was all too real. And deep down, he knew the Shadow Eater wasn't just feeding on fear.

It was growing stronger.

Chapter 8: The Monster's Evolution

The morning sunlight in Hollow Creek brought no comfort. It was a weak, pale light that seemed incapable of dispelling the growing darkness that hung over the town like a shroud. The streets were eerily quiet, dotted with abandoned cars and empty homes. Only a handful of stubborn residents remained, barricaded inside, praying they wouldn't be next.

Sheriff Caleb Morgan leaned against his cruiser, his eyes scanning the treeline at the edge of the Blackthorn Forest. He hadn't slept in over twenty-four hours, and it was starting to show. His beard was unkempt, his uniform rumpled, and his usual calm demeanor was cracking under the weight of mounting terror.

"Sheriff," Deputy Carla Hensley called, jogging over from the station. "Another call just came in. Daylight attack."

Morgan stiffened, pushing off the car. "Where?"

"Old Miller's farm," Carla replied, catching her breath. "Neighbor saw it happen. Said it wasn't just a shadow anymore. Said it... had a face."

Morgan felt a chill crawl down his spine. "Get in the car."

They sped down the dusty road to the Miller farm, the cruiser kicking up clouds of dirt. When they arrived, they found Ruth Baker, the elderly neighbor, sitting on the porch of her farmhouse. She clutched a rosary in her hands, her knuckles white.

"Mrs. Baker," Morgan said, stepping out of the car. "What did you see?"

Ruth looked up at him, her face pale and streaked with tears. "It... it wasn't just a shadow anymore," she whispered, her voice trembling. "It had arms, legs, a head... but not like anything human. And its face—" She choked on a sob. "Its face was all wrong."

Morgan crouched beside her, his tone gentle but urgent. "What do you mean by 'wrong,' ma'am?"

"It wasn't just one face," Ruth said, her eyes wide with terror. "It was many. I saw Miller's face, and his wife's, and others I didn't recognize. Like it was wearing them, overlapping, shifting…"

Carla exchanged a look with Morgan. "Did it… speak?" she asked hesitantly.

Ruth nodded. "Not words. Just a sound, like a low growl mixed with a scream. It came out of every face, all at once."

Morgan straightened, his jaw tight. "Where did it go?"

Ruth pointed toward the treeline. "Back into the woods."

The Millers' farmhouse was eerily silent as Morgan and Carla approached. The door was ajar, creaking in the breeze. Morgan pushed it open with his flashlight, his other hand on his holstered weapon.

The scene inside was horrific. Furniture was overturned, the walls were streaked with blood, and deep claw marks marred the floorboards. In the center of the living room lay two bodies—Old Miller and his wife. Their faces were frozen in expressions of sheer terror, their skin unnaturally pale, as if drained of all color.

Carla swallowed hard, covering her mouth. "Jesus…"

Morgan crouched to inspect the bodies. "Same as the others. No blood left, no signs of a struggle. It's like they didn't even fight back."

Carla shuddered. "Or didn't have the strength to."

Morgan's flashlight beam caught something on the wall—a large, circular scorch mark. He stepped closer, noticing that the edges seemed to shimmer faintly, as if the air itself had been warped.

"What do you make of this?" he asked.

Carla shook her head. "I don't know, but it's not natural."

Morgan sighed, running a hand through his hair. "Let's call Emily. She needs to see this."

Dr. Emily Carson arrived an hour later, her car packed with books and equipment. She stepped inside the farmhouse, her face grim as she took in the scene.

"It's evolving," she said after examining the scorch mark. "Each kill makes it stronger, more corporeal. It's absorbing the essence of its victims—everything that made them who they were."

"Essence?" Carla asked, frowning. "You mean their souls?"

Emily nodded. "If you want to put it in spiritual terms, yes. Their life force, their memories, even their identities. That's why it's starting to take on a form. It's no longer just a shadow."

Morgan crossed his arms. "And now it's bold enough to attack during the day. What does that mean for us?"

"It means it's getting harder to stop," Emily replied. "The more it feeds, the less it's bound by the rules of our world. Soon, it won't need the darkness at all."

Later that day, Morgan called an emergency meeting at Town Hall. The remaining residents—now fewer than fifty—gathered in the dimly lit auditorium, their faces etched with fear. Emily stood beside him, clutching her notes.

"Listen up," Morgan said, his voice carrying over the murmurs. "The situation has changed. The attacks are happening during the day now, and the creature is getting stronger. If you haven't left town yet, I strongly suggest you do so immediately."

"What about those of us who can't leave?" an elderly man called from the back. "This is our home!"

Morgan's expression softened. "I understand. And we're doing everything we can to stop this thing. But you have to understand—it's not safe here anymore."

Emily stepped forward. "We believe the creature is feeding off fear and despair. The more people are afraid, the stronger it becomes. If you stay, you must remain calm and avoid feeding into its power."

"That's easy for you to say," a young woman snapped. "You're not the one with a monster outside your window!"

Morgan raised his hands to calm the crowd. "We're working on a plan. In the meantime, lock your doors, stay indoors, and call us if you see anything unusual."

That night, as Morgan and Carla patrolled the streets, they noticed the silence. No birds, no insects, no rustling leaves—just an oppressive stillness that made the hair on the back of Morgan's neck stand up.

"Do you feel that?" Carla asked, gripping the wheel tightly.

"Yeah," Morgan replied, scanning the darkness with his flashlight. "It's too quiet."

They turned a corner and saw it—a dark, hulking figure standing in the middle of the street. Its body seemed to ripple, shifting between solid and shadow, and its face... its face was a grotesque patchwork of its victims, their features merging and overlapping in a horrifying mosaic.

Carla slammed on the brakes, her eyes wide. "Is that...?"

Morgan drew his weapon, stepping out of the car. "Stay here."

"Sheriff, don't—" Carla started, but he was already moving forward.

The creature turned its many faces toward him, its glowing red eyes locking onto his. It let out a guttural growl, a sound that seemed to vibrate the air around it. Morgan stopped, his weapon trembling in his hands.

"Go back to the darkness," he said, his voice steady despite the fear gnawing at him. "You're not welcome here."

The creature tilted its head, its faces shifting and merging. Then, without warning, it lunged, its form stretching unnaturally as it closed the distance.

"Run!" Morgan shouted, firing his weapon.

The bullets passed through the creature, tearing into the pavement behind it. It let out a deafening screech, and the air around it grew icy cold. Morgan stumbled back, barely making it into the cruiser before Carla hit the gas.

"What the hell was that?" she shouted as they sped away.

"Something we can't kill," Morgan said, his voice grim. "Not with bullets."

As they drove into the night, the creature watched them go, its many faces contorted into a twisted mockery of a smile. It was stronger now, and it knew they couldn't stop it. Not yet.

Chapter 9: Fighting the Unfathomable

Sheriff Caleb Morgan's office was no longer a place of quiet paperwork and mundane police business. Maps of Hollow Creek and its surrounding areas were spread across the desks, dotted with pins marking attack sites. Notes scrawled in desperation covered every available surface, and the air smelled of stale coffee and adrenaline. This was now a war room.

Dr. Emily Carson stood at the center, flipping through a thick leather-bound book filled with esoteric symbols and handwritten notes. Her brow was furrowed in concentration, and her lips moved silently as she read. Around her stood the few people brave—or desperate—enough to stay and fight: Carla Hensley, Mayor Evelyn Grayson, and three townsfolk who had refused to abandon their homes.

"This has to work," Evelyn said, her arms crossed. The usually composed mayor now looked haggard, her blazer wrinkled and her face pale. "We've tried everything else."

"It's not that simple," Emily replied, looking up from the book. "This creature isn't bound by the physical laws we understand. It's older than anything in our history, and it thrives on fear and despair. Every failed attempt makes it stronger."

Morgan stood by the window, staring out at the empty streets. The once-bustling town was now a ghost town, its remaining residents barricaded inside their homes. He turned to the group, his expression grim.

"Let's go over the list again," he said. "What've we tried so far?"

Carla grabbed a clipboard and began rattling off the methods. "Silver bullets—no effect. Fire—it seems to dissipate temporarily but comes back stronger. Salt barriers around properties—useless. Holy water, prayers, chants—nothing."

"What about the rituals?" asked Joe Wilkes, the retired logger who had seen the Shadow Eater years ago. He clutched his axe like a lifeline, his knuckles white.

"We've tried two of the simpler ones," Emily said, flipping to a marked page in her book. "Neither had any effect. They were likely meant for lesser entities, not something of this magnitude."

"What's left?" Morgan asked, his voice edged with frustration.

Emily hesitated before answering. "There's one more ritual. It's... complicated, and it requires a conduit—a person willing to act as a bridge between the Shadow Eater's realm and ours."

"What happens to the conduit?" Carla asked, already dreading the answer.

Emily looked away. "They don't survive."

The room fell silent, the weight of her words settling over them like a suffocating blanket.

"We're not there yet," Morgan finally said, his tone resolute. "There has to be another way."

Evelyn sighed. "We don't have much time, Caleb. Every day, this thing grows stronger. If we wait too long, there won't be anyone left to save."

"Then we'll find another way," Morgan said firmly. "We're not sacrificing anyone until we've exhausted every option."

Emily nodded reluctantly. "There are a few more theories we can test. But we need to act quickly."

That night, the group gathered at the abandoned high school gymnasium, which they had repurposed as a testing ground. Morgan had ordered the space cleared and fortified, and the floors were marked with protective sigils and salt lines. The Shadow Eater's most recent attack had been nearby, and they hoped to lure it into a controlled confrontation.

"Everything's ready," Carla said, double-checking the salt lines. "We've got fire, silver, holy water, and a modified version of one of the rituals Emily found."

"Good," Morgan replied, his hand resting on his holstered weapon. "If this thing shows up, we hit it with everything we've got."

Joe stood near the back of the gym, his axe at the ready. "You really think this is gonna work?"

"It has to," Morgan said, though his voice lacked conviction.

Hours passed, and the gym was silent except for the occasional creak of the building settling. The air grew colder, and a faint, unnatural darkness began to seep into the corners of the room.

"It's here," Emily whispered, clutching her book tightly.

The darkness coalesced into the now-familiar form of the Shadow Eater. Its body was a writhing mass of shadows, and its grotesque, shifting faces glared at them with glowing red eyes. It moved with unnatural fluidity, its limbs stretching and twisting as it advanced.

"Now!" Morgan shouted.

Carla threw a vial of holy water at the creature, which sizzled on contact but didn't slow it down. Joe swung his axe, but it passed harmlessly through the shadowy form. Evelyn lit a Molotov cocktail and hurled it at the creature, engulfing it in flames. For a moment, it shrieked and writhed, but the fire extinguished itself unnaturally fast, and the creature surged forward, more aggressive than before.

"It's not working!" Carla yelled, backing away.

Emily began chanting in a trembling voice, reciting the words from her book. The sigils on the floor glowed faintly, and the creature paused, its many faces twisting in what almost looked like pain. But then it let out a deafening screech, and the glow faded.

"The ritual's not strong enough!" Emily cried. "It's feeding off our fear—stay calm!"

"Stay calm?" Joe shouted. "That thing's gonna kill us!"

The Shadow Eater lunged, its shadowy limbs slamming into the protective salt lines and scattering them. Morgan fired his weapon, each shot echoing uselessly in the gym. The creature's screech grew louder, and the temperature plummeted.

"Fall back!" Morgan shouted, grabbing Carla and pulling her toward the exit.

Emily clutched her book and followed, her breath visible in the freezing air. Joe hesitated, swinging his axe one last time before retreating with the others. The creature didn't pursue them. Instead, it stood in the center of the gym, its many faces contorted into mocking smiles as it dissolved back into the darkness.

The group reconvened at the sheriff's office, their faces pale and their spirits crushed.

"That thing's unstoppable," Joe said, slumping into a chair. "It's like it gets stronger every time we hit it."

Emily set her book down with a heavy sigh. "It's not just physical attacks. Every failed attempt feeds its confidence—and our fear."

"So what now?" Carla asked, her voice trembling. "If nothing works, what's the point?"

Morgan leaned against his desk, his jaw tight. "We don't give up. We regroup, come up with a new plan."

Evelyn shook her head. "Caleb, we're running out of time. If we don't stop it soon, there won't be anything left to fight for."

Morgan met her gaze, his eyes burning with determination. "Then we keep fighting. Because if we stop, that thing wins."

The room fell silent, the only sound the faint rustle of pages as Emily flipped through her book again. Outside, the wind howled, carrying with it the faint, guttural growl of the Shadow Eater.

The battle was far from over, but Morgan refused to let despair take hold. As long as they still had breath, they would fight the unfathomable—even if it meant standing on the edge of oblivion.

Chapter 10: The Sacrifice

The library was silent except for the faint hum of the overhead lights and the occasional turning of a page. Dr. Emily Carson sat at a long wooden table, her brow furrowed in concentration. The book before her was ancient, its brittle pages yellowed and filled with cryptic text in a language few could decipher. Her notebook was filled with translations and annotations, the culmination of sleepless nights and desperate hope.

Sheriff Caleb Morgan and Deputy Carla Hensley sat across from her, their expressions tense. Joe Wilkes leaned against a nearby bookshelf, his axe still in hand, while Mayor Evelyn Grayson stood near the window, staring out at the deserted streets.

"Anything?" Morgan asked, breaking the heavy silence.

Emily looked up, her green eyes weary but determined. "I think I've found something."

The group straightened, the room suddenly alive with nervous anticipation.

"There's a ritual," Emily began, her voice steady despite the weight of her words. "It's more powerful than the others we've tried. It's designed to sever the Shadow Eater's connection to our plane entirely. But..."

Morgan narrowed his eyes. "But what?"

"It requires a conduit," Emily said, her tone heavy. "A living sacrifice of pure intent. Someone who's willing to offer their life freely, without hesitation or fear."

The room fell silent, the enormity of her words sinking in. Carla was the first to speak.

"Sacrifice?" she repeated, her voice rising. "You mean someone has to die?"

Emily nodded solemnly. "The Shadow Eater is an ancient entity, bound by equally ancient rules. It can't be destroyed by force, but it can be banished. The conduit becomes a bridge, channeling the entity's power back into the void where it came from."

"That's insane," Joe said, his grip tightening on his axe. "We can't ask someone to do that."

"We might not have a choice," Emily replied. "If we don't act soon, the Shadow Eater will grow too strong to contain."

Morgan leaned back in his chair, his expression unreadable. "And how exactly do we find someone willing to sacrifice themselves?"

The answer came unexpectedly.

"I'll do it," a soft voice said.

The group turned to see Grace Harper standing in the doorway. She was a young woman, barely twenty, with auburn hair that framed her delicate face. Her eyes, though tired, burned with quiet determination.

"Grace," Morgan said, his tone cautious. "You don't have to—"

"Yes, I do," she interrupted, stepping into the room. "I've seen what that thing can do. It took my little brother. If I can stop it, if I can save someone else's family, then it's worth it."

Evelyn shook her head. "You're just a kid. This isn't your fight."

"It's everyone's fight," Grace said firmly. "And I'm not afraid."

The room erupted into a flurry of arguments. Carla begged Grace to reconsider, while Joe muttered angrily about how they shouldn't even be considering the ritual. Evelyn looked as though she might be sick, and Morgan sat silently, his gaze fixed on the table.

Finally, Emily raised her voice. "Enough!"

The room fell quiet, and all eyes turned to her.

"This isn't our decision to make," Emily said, her tone resolute. "The ritual requires pure intent. If Grace is willing to do this, it has to be her choice."

Morgan stood, his expression grim. "Grace, do you understand what this means? There's no coming back from this."

"I understand," Grace said, her voice unwavering. "And I'm ready."

Preparations for the ritual began immediately. Emily worked tirelessly to ensure every detail was correct, from the placement of the sigils to the specific incantations. The ritual would take place in the heart of the Blackthorn Forest, where the Shadow Eater's presence was strongest.

The group accompanied Grace to the site at dusk, the air heavy with foreboding. She wore a simple white dress, and her auburn hair shimmered in the fading light. Despite the gravity of the situation, she seemed calm.

"Are you scared?" Carla asked softly as they walked.

Grace smiled faintly. "A little. But not for me. I'm scared it won't work."

"It'll work," Carla said, her voice breaking. "It has to."

At the ritual site, Emily drew a large circle on the ground, surrounding it with intricate symbols and runes. Candles were placed at precise intervals, their flickering flames the only light in the gathering darkness. Grace stood at the center, her hands clasped in front of her.

"Remember," Emily said, addressing the group. "No matter what happens, no one can enter the circle. If the ritual is interrupted, it could make the Shadow Eater even stronger."

Morgan nodded, his hand resting on his weapon. "We'll cover you."

Emily stepped into the circle, standing beside Grace. She opened her book and began to chant, her voice steady and melodic. The symbols on the ground began to glow faintly, and the air grew colder.

Suddenly, the shadows around them began to writhe and coalesce, forming the monstrous shape of the Shadow Eater. Its many faces twisted in fury, and its guttural growl echoed through the forest.

"It's here," Emily whispered.

Grace took a deep breath and stepped forward. "I'm ready."

As Emily continued the chant, Grace knelt in the center of the circle, her hands resting on the glowing sigils. The Shadow Eater lunged toward her, but the circle held, the symbols flaring brightly as it was repelled.

Grace closed her eyes, her voice steady as she began to speak. "I offer myself freely. Take my life, my light, and leave this world in peace."

The Shadow Eater screeched, its many faces contorted in agony. The ground beneath the circle trembled, and the glowing symbols grew brighter, blindingly so.

"Grace!" Carla cried, stepping forward, but Morgan held her back.

"No," he said firmly. "We can't interfere."

Grace's body began to shimmer, her outline blurring as the light from the symbols enveloped her. The Shadow Eater let out one final, deafening shriek before its form dissolved into darkness, sucked into the void.

When the light faded, Grace was gone. The circle was empty, the symbols scorched into the ground as a permanent reminder of her sacrifice.

The group stood in silence, the weight of what had just happened settling over them. Carla wiped tears from her eyes, and even Joe looked shaken.

"She did it," Evelyn said softly, her voice trembling. "She stopped it."

Morgan nodded, his throat tight. "Yeah. She did."

As they left the forest, the first rays of dawn broke through the trees, bathing the town in a light that felt brighter and warmer than it had in weeks. Grace's sacrifice had ended the nightmare, but it was a victory that would haunt them forever.

Chapter 11: The Final Stand

The quarry was a bleak, lifeless expanse on the outskirts of Hollow Creek, its jagged walls towering like a natural amphitheater of despair. The ground was uneven, littered with rocks and debris, and a bitter wind howled through the hollow space. It was the perfect place for a trap—isolated, inescapable, and far enough from the remaining townsfolk to avoid collateral damage.

Sheriff Caleb Morgan stood at the edge of the quarry, his breath visible in the cold night air. He surveyed the makeshift battlefield below, where Dr. Emily Carson was meticulously drawing the ritual circle in white chalk, her movements precise despite the urgency of the moment. Deputy Carla Hensley and the remaining survivors—Joe Wilkes, Mayor Evelyn Grayson, and two others—were setting up the final elements: torches, salt lines, and crude barricades.

"This has to work," Carla said, adjusting her flashlight as she placed a salt canister on the ground. "If it doesn't…"

Morgan didn't let her finish. "It will," he said firmly, though his tone carried the weight of doubt. "We don't have another choice."

Emily looked up from her work, her face pale but determined. "The circle is ready," she said. "Everything is in place."

"Talk me through it again," Morgan said, stepping closer.

Emily nodded. "The ritual is designed to sever the Shadow Eater's connection to our world. Grace's sacrifice weakened it, but this will finish the job. The incantation must be spoken from within the circle, uninterrupted. Once the creature is inside, the symbols will trap it. It will resist—violently—but the circle should hold if it's drawn correctly."

"And if it doesn't?" Joe asked, gripping his axe tightly.

Emily hesitated. "Then we don't survive the night."

The bait for the Shadow Eater was simple but effective. A bright bonfire burned in the center of the quarry, its flickering light drawing shadows against the walls. The survivors stood at strategic points around the circle, armed with everything they could muster: weapons, fire, and sheer desperation. Morgan took his place near Emily, his shotgun loaded with silver-infused shells, even though he knew they'd be useless against the creature.

The wait was agonizing. Minutes stretched into what felt like hours, the oppressive silence broken only by the crackling of the fire and the occasional gust of wind.

Then it came.

A wave of cold washed over the quarry, extinguishing the torches one by one. The bonfire flickered, its flames dimming as an unnatural darkness seeped into the edges of the circle. The Shadow Eater appeared, its grotesque form writhing and shifting like liquid smoke. Its many faces glared at them with glowing red eyes, their expressions a grotesque mix of rage and torment.

"It's here," Emily whispered, clutching the ancient book tightly.

Morgan raised his shotgun. "Everyone, hold your positions."

The creature let out a guttural growl, its sound reverberating through the quarry like a physical force. It lunged toward the bonfire, but as it crossed the edge of the ritual circle, the symbols flared to life, glowing with an intense white light. The Shadow Eater recoiled, screeching in pain.

"It's working!" Carla shouted, but her triumph was short-lived.

The Shadow Eater began to lash out, its shadowy limbs slamming against the glowing barrier. The ground trembled, and cracks spider-webbed through the circle. The survivors braced themselves as rocks tumbled from the quarry walls.

"Emily, start the chant!" Morgan yelled.

Emily opened the book and began to chant, her voice steady despite the chaos around her. The words were ancient and melodic, carrying a resonance that seemed to pierce the unnatural cold. The symbols in the circle pulsed in time with her words, and the Shadow Eater writhed, its form distorting as if it were being pulled apart.

The creature let out a deafening screech and turned its fury on the survivors. A shadowy tendril shot toward Joe, wrapping around his torso and lifting him into the air.

"Joe!" Carla screamed, firing her pistol at the tendril, but the bullets passed through harmlessly.

Joe's screams were cut short as the tendril tightened, crushing him. His body fell to the ground, lifeless.

"Stay focused!" Morgan shouted, his voice hoarse. "Don't let it break the circle!"

The Shadow Eater continued its assault, its tendrils sweeping through the quarry like a hurricane. One of the townsfolk, a young man named Kyle, was struck by a shadowy appendage and thrown into the quarry wall with bone-shattering force. Evelyn barely managed to dive out of the way as another tendril smashed into her barricade, scattering rocks and salt.

Emily's voice wavered but didn't falter. "I'm almost there! Keep it distracted!"

Morgan fired his shotgun, the silver shells momentarily disrupting one of the tendrils. "You heard her! Light it up!"

Carla grabbed a Molotov cocktail, lit the rag, and hurled it at the creature. The flames engulfed part of its form, causing it to thrash and scream, but the fire didn't last long. The creature's faces twisted in fury as it redoubled its efforts to break free.

As Emily neared the final lines of the incantation, the Shadow Eater made one last, desperate move. It surged toward her, its entire form collapsing into a single, massive tendril that slammed against the circle's barrier. The glowing symbols flickered and dimmed, and for a terrifying moment, it seemed as though the circle would fail.

Morgan didn't hesitate. He stepped into the circle, his shotgun raised, and fired directly into the creature's face. The shot didn't harm it, but it drew its attention away from Emily.

"Finish it!" Morgan shouted. "Now!"

Emily shouted the final words of the incantation, her voice ringing out over the chaos. The symbols flared brighter than ever, and a blinding column of light erupted from the circle, enveloping the Shadow Eater. The creature screeched, its form twisting and disintegrating as the light consumed it.

The survivors shielded their eyes as the light grew brighter and brighter, and then, as suddenly as it had appeared, it was gone.

Silence fell over the quarry. The air was still, and the oppressive cold had vanished. The Shadow Eater was no more.

Morgan helped Emily to her feet, her face pale but relieved. Carla stood nearby, her hands trembling as she stared at the empty circle.

"Is it... is it over?" Evelyn asked, her voice barely a whisper.

Emily nodded. "It's over."

Morgan looked around at the survivors—what was left of them. Joe was gone, along with Kyle and another brave soul who had stayed to fight. The price of victory had been steep, but they had won.

As they climbed out of the quarry, the first light of dawn broke over the horizon. For the first time in weeks, the sun felt warm, and the shadows no longer seemed alive.

Hollow Creek was free, but the scars of their battle would remain forever.

Chapter 12: The Cost

The morning after the battle at the quarry, a heavy fog blanketed Hollow Creek. The streets were eerily quiet, the kind of silence that pressed into the ears and sank into the bones. Sheriff Caleb Morgan walked the deserted main road, his boots crunching on broken glass and debris. Hollow Creek was no longer the town he had sworn to protect. It was a graveyard.

Windows were shattered, doors hung off their hinges, and once-busy storefronts stood abandoned. The air carried the faint, acrid smell of smoke, mingling with the metallic tang of dried blood. Morgan's eyes scanned the remnants of his home—an overturned bench at the park, a child's bicycle lying forgotten in the gutter. Every inch of the town bore the marks of devastation.

The survivors gathered at the community center, now a makeshift shelter. There were only a handful left: Morgan, Deputy Carla Hensley, Dr. Emily Carson, Mayor Evelyn Grayson, and a few others who had refused to flee or hadn't had the chance. Their faces were drawn, their eyes hollow.

Evelyn sat at a folding table, her head in her hands. "We lost so much," she said, her voice barely audible. "The people, the town... everything."

Morgan stood nearby, leaning against the wall, his arms crossed. "We're still here," he said, though even he couldn't summon much conviction. "That counts for something."

"Does it?" Evelyn snapped, lifting her head to glare at him. "Look around, Caleb. Hollow Creek is gone. We might've stopped that... thing, but at what cost?"

Carla stepped forward, her voice firm but gentle. "We stopped it from spreading. Grace's sacrifice saved more than just us. It saved thousands—millions—beyond this town."

Evelyn's eyes softened, and she nodded, though the pain remained etched on her face. "You're right. I know you're right. But it doesn't make it any easier."

Emily stood by the window, gazing out at the fog-shrouded streets. "The Shadow Eater is gone," she said, more to herself than to anyone else. "But its scars will linger. Not just here, but in every place it touched."

Morgan turned to her. "What do you mean?"

Emily hesitated before answering. "The Shadow Eater feeds on fear, despair, and death. Even though we banished it, the echoes of what it did remain. People will feel it—the lingering darkness. And then there's what it said."

The room fell silent.

"It spoke?" Carla asked, her voice barely above a whisper.

Emily nodded. "As it was being destroyed, it said, 'I will return.'"

The weight of her words hung heavy in the air. Morgan clenched his fists, his jaw tightening. "If it does, we'll stop it again."

Emily turned to face him, her expression grave. "If it comes back, Sheriff, it won't be the same. It learns, it adapts. Next time, it may not be something we can fight."

The survivors spent the following days trying to rebuild, though the effort was half-hearted at best. The town was too broken, and the population too decimated. Homes were empty, and businesses remained shuttered. The people who stayed did so out of necessity, not hope.

Carla helped organize supplies, distributing food and blankets to the few remaining families. She moved with a determined efficiency, but her hands shook when she thought no one was watching.

"Carla," Morgan said one afternoon as they worked side by side, unloading a crate of canned goods. "You doing okay?"

She paused, taking a deep breath. "I don't know," she admitted. "Every time I close my eyes, I see it. The faces, the screams... Joe, Grace... everyone we lost."

Morgan placed a hand on her shoulder. "You're not alone. None of us are."

Carla nodded, though tears welled in her eyes. "It doesn't feel that way sometimes."

Dr. Emily Carson threw herself into her research, hoping to make sense of what they had faced. She spent hours in the library, poring over texts and journals, trying to understand how such a creature could exist—and whether it could truly be gone.

Evelyn, meanwhile, focused on securing resources for the survivors. She spent her days on the phone, pleading with state officials and aid organizations for help. Hollow Creek was no longer a priority for anyone outside its borders, and she knew it.

"Do they even care?" she asked Morgan one evening, slamming the phone down. "We're just another forgotten tragedy to them."

Morgan shook his head. "We care. That's enough."

Evelyn looked at him, her eyes filled with a mixture of exhaustion and gratitude. "You're a good man, Caleb. But this town needs more than just us."

One night, as the survivors gathered around a fire outside the community center, Grace's name came up. It was Carla who spoke first.

"She didn't hesitate," Carla said, staring into the flames. "She just... stepped forward. Like she knew it was her purpose."

Joe's widow, Mary, nodded slowly. "Grace saved us all. We owe her everything."

"We owe her more than we can ever repay," Morgan said, his voice heavy. "She gave up her life so the rest of us could live."

Emily looked down at her hands, guilt flickering across her face. "I hate that it had to be her. That we couldn't find another way."

Morgan met her gaze. "She made her choice, Emily. And it wasn't just for us. It was for everyone. She knew what was at stake."

The fire crackled, and for a moment, the group sat in solemn silence.

In the weeks that followed, most of the survivors left Hollow Creek, seeking new lives far from the shadows of the past. Morgan stayed, refusing to abandon the town he had spent his life protecting. Carla stayed with him, and together they patrolled the empty streets, more out of habit than necessity.

Emily eventually packed her things and left as well, though not before leaving Morgan a box of her research. "Just in case," she said softly.

As she drove away, Morgan watched her car disappear into the distance. The weight of everything they had endured settled on his shoulders, heavier than ever.

One evening, months later, Morgan stood at the edge of the Blackthorn Forest, staring into the darkness. The town was quiet, and the wind whispered through the trees.

"I will return."

The Shadow Eater's final words echoed in his mind, a chilling reminder of the fragile peace they had won. Morgan tightened his grip on his flashlight and stepped back toward the town.

The battle was over, but the war against the darkness was far from finished. Hollow Creek might never be the same, but as long as he drew breath, Caleb Morgan would be ready.

Chapter 13: Rebuilding the World

The events in Hollow Creek left scars far beyond the confines of the small town. News of the catastrophe, distorted and reshaped by rumor and misinformation, spread across the globe like wildfire. Footage from the viral video of Mark Hayes, witness accounts, and eerie reports of shadowy figures had sparked a frenzy of speculation.

Governments, scrambling to maintain order, issued statements dismissing the incident as a "localized hysteria exacerbated by social media." Experts were trotted out on major news networks to declare the Shadow Eater a fabrication, a psychological phenomenon born of fear and collective delusion. But for those who had survived the nightmare, the truth was undeniable—and it was terrifying.

Sheriff Caleb Morgan sat at a desk in the empty Hollow Creek sheriff's office, flipping through a stack of papers and reports. Most were mundane—requests for missing persons, scattered aid applications—but a few were far from ordinary. Letters and emails from people across the world who claimed to have experienced something similar to the Shadow Eater's attacks: dark figures in the corners of their rooms, suffocating cold, and whispers in the dead of night.

"This can't just be us," Morgan muttered, setting the papers aside.

Deputy Carla Hensley walked in, carrying a cup of coffee and a laptop. "It's not," she said, setting the laptop down in front of him. "Look at this."

Morgan scrolled through the screen, his frown deepening as he read. Forums and social media posts were ablaze with conspiracy theories. People were sharing grainy photos of claw marks on walls, videos of unexplained power outages, and accounts of entire neighborhoods falling eerily silent.

"They're calling it 'The Shadow Pandemic,'" Carla said. "Because it's spreading, just like fear."

Morgan rubbed his temples. "And the government's still calling it a hoax?"

Carla nodded. "Yep. Official story is it was some kind of mass hallucination fueled by hysteria and fake videos. They've even pulled the Hayes video from most platforms."

"But it's still out there," Morgan said, scrolling to a re-upload of the viral video. "People know what they saw."

In Washington D.C., a closed-door meeting of high-ranking officials was underway. The room was dimly lit, and the atmosphere was tense. A representative from a shadowy intelligence agency stood at the head of the table, addressing the group.

"The Hollow Creek incident is officially classified as a national security threat," the man said, his tone clipped. "We cannot allow this kind of hysteria to undermine public confidence. The official narrative remains unchanged: localized hysteria, no credible evidence of supernatural phenomena."

"And what about the survivors?" asked a senator, leaning forward. "The ones who claim they fought some... entity?"

"They've been dismissed as unreliable witnesses," the man replied. "Their accounts are being discredited as part of the psychological fallout from a natural disaster."

Another senator shook her head. "Do you really think that will work? The footage, the stories—they're spreading too fast."

The man's expression darkened. "We have contingencies. The truth must not get out."

Back in Hollow Creek, Dr. Emily Carson returned to the town for the first time since leaving. She had spent months traveling, meeting with others who had encountered the Shadow Eater or similar entities. Her research was expanding, and her determination to prepare for the entity's return had only grown stronger.

She entered the sheriff's office to find Morgan and Carla hunched over maps and reports. "You're still fighting," she said, a small smile touching her lips.

"Someone has to," Morgan replied, gesturing for her to sit. "What did you find?"

Emily pulled out a thick binder and spread its contents on the desk. "The Shadow Eater isn't unique. I've found records of similar entities in ancient texts—some in Europe, others in Asia, even the Americas. They go by different names, but the descriptions are eerily consistent."

"Any idea how to stop them permanently?" Carla asked.

Emily hesitated. "The rituals we used in Hollow Creek worked because of Grace's sacrifice, but there's no guarantee they'd work again. These entities adapt. They learn."

Morgan frowned. "So what are you saying? Next time, we might not have a chance?"

Emily nodded reluctantly. "Unless we can find a way to understand their origins, their weaknesses, we'll always be one step behind."

Meanwhile, survivors from Hollow Creek and other affected areas began forming secret networks. Using encrypted messaging apps and hidden forums, they shared information, tips, and theories about how to protect themselves and prepare for future encounters.

One such group, calling themselves "The Lightkeepers," met in a remote cabin deep in the Appalachian Mountains. Around a flickering lantern, they discussed strategies for survival.

"We need to stockpile supplies—salt, holy water, anything we can use to protect ourselves," said a burly man with a scar running down his cheek.

"And we need to spread the word," said a woman with dark circles under her eyes. "The government won't warn people, so we have to."

"But we can't panic them," another man interjected. "The more fear there is, the stronger these things get."

The group nodded solemnly, their resolve hardening. They knew the battle wasn't over—it was only just beginning.

Back in Hollow Creek, Morgan and Emily stood on the edge of the Blackthorn Forest, staring into the fading light of dusk.

"It feels different," Emily said, her voice barely above a whisper.

Morgan nodded. "Quieter. Like it's waiting."

"You think it'll come back here?" she asked.

"I don't know," Morgan admitted. "But if it does, we'll be ready."

Emily glanced at him. "You really believe that?"

Morgan turned to her, his expression resolute. "I have to. For Grace. For everyone we lost."

As the sun dipped below the horizon, the shadows lengthened, but this time, they seemed less oppressive. The survivors of Hollow Creek carried the weight of their scars, but they also carried something else: hope. Hope that, no matter how dark the night, the light could always return.

And if the Shadow Eater did come back, they would be ready to face it—together.

Chapter 14: The Echo

The faint hum of fluorescent lights flickered in the empty hallway of the Hollow Creek sheriff's office. Sheriff Caleb Morgan sat at his desk, staring at a pile of reports that shouldn't have existed. Power outages in homes with no discernible cause, unexplained cold spots in the town's outskirts, and eyewitness accounts of shifting shadows.

Morgan pinched the bridge of his nose, exhaustion weighing on him like a lead blanket. The events of the past months had taken their toll. He had convinced himself—and what little remained of the town—that the nightmare was over. That Grace's sacrifice had brought peace. But the reports said otherwise.

A soft knock at the door broke his reverie. Deputy Carla Hensley stepped in, holding a stack of papers and a tired expression.

"More of them," she said, dropping the papers onto his desk. "A farmer out by Ridgeway says his entire herd of cattle vanished overnight. No tracks, no signs of predators—just gone."

Morgan looked up at her, his jaw tightening. "And the lights?"

"Flickering on and off in the middle of the night," Carla confirmed. "Same pattern as before. They're reporting it in Ridgeway, Fairview, and even as far as Hollow Bend."

Morgan stood, pacing the room. "This doesn't make sense. We stopped it. We saw it die."

Carla folded her arms, her voice low. "Maybe we didn't stop it entirely."

Later that day, Morgan and Carla drove out to the edge of Blackthorn Forest. The trees stood tall and ominous, their shadows stretching across the ground like skeletal fingers. The area was quiet—too quiet.

"This place still gives me the creeps," Carla muttered, her hand resting on her holstered sidearm.

Morgan scanned the treeline with narrowed eyes. "You feel that?"

Carla nodded. The air was colder here, the kind of chill that seeped into your bones and made the hairs on your neck stand on end.

They walked deeper into the forest, their footsteps muffled by the thick carpet of leaves. Morgan paused when he noticed something on the ground—a journal, its leather cover scuffed and weathered. He knelt to pick it up, brushing away the dirt.

"It's Emily's," he said, flipping it open. The pages were filled with her meticulous handwriting, diagrams of ritual circles, and notes on the Shadow Eater. Toward the end of the journal, the writing became frantic, the sentences disjointed.

Carla leaned over his shoulder, reading aloud. "It was never truly gone. Its essence lingers, waiting, feeding."

Morgan's heart sank as he turned to the final entry. The words were scrawled in large, uneven letters: *It's coming back.*

Back at the sheriff's office, Morgan spread the journal across his desk, pouring over Emily's final notes. Carla sat nearby, flipping through her own stack of reports.

"Listen to this," Morgan said, reading aloud. "She wrote: 'The Shadow Eater is a fragment of something larger. Destroying its physical form didn't end it—it only severed part of its connection. The rest remains.'"

Carla frowned. "The rest? What does that even mean?"

"It means we didn't finish the job," Morgan said, his voice grim. "We cut off the head, but the body's still out there."

The phone on Morgan's desk rang, startling them both. He picked it up, and the shaky voice on the other end made his stomach drop.

"Sheriff... it's back," the caller whispered. "I saw it. In my house. It was in the shadows..."

"Who is this?" Morgan asked, his voice urgent.

"Bill. Bill Kline," the man replied. "You've gotta come quick. It's—" The line went dead, leaving only a faint static.

Morgan slammed the phone down. "Kline's farm. Let's go."

The drive to Bill Kline's farm was tense. The sun was setting, casting the sky in shades of orange and red. By the time they arrived, the property was shrouded in twilight, the farmhouse eerily dark.

"Bill!" Morgan called as they stepped out of the cruiser. "It's the sheriff!"

There was no response. The front door creaked open, swaying in the wind. Morgan and Carla exchanged a glance before drawing their weapons and stepping inside.

The house was cold, the kind of cold that froze breath midair. Shadows danced across the walls, shifting unnaturally as if alive. Morgan's flashlight beam swept across the room, revealing overturned furniture and broken glass.

"Sheriff..." Carla whispered, pointing to the floor.

A large, circular scorch mark marred the wooden planks, the same kind they had seen at every attack site. Morgan's grip on his flashlight tightened.

"Bill?" he called again, his voice echoing through the empty house.

A faint growl resonated from upstairs, low and guttural. Carla raised her weapon, her eyes wide. "What the hell was that?"

Morgan motioned for her to follow as they ascended the creaking staircase. The growl grew louder, more menacing. At the top of the stairs, the air was suffocatingly cold. The shadows thickened, converging at the end of the hallway.

And then they saw it.

The Shadow Eater, or what was left of it, loomed at the far end of the hall. Its form was smaller, more fragmented, but no less terrifying. Faces flickered across its surface, their expressions frozen in silent screams.

"Get back!" Morgan shouted, firing his weapon.

The bullets passed through the creature, leaving it unfazed. It lunged toward them, a shadowy tendril whipping through the air. Morgan and Carla dove out of the way as the tendril struck the wall, leaving deep, jagged grooves.

"We can't fight this!" Carla yelled, scrambling to her feet.

"We have to try!" Morgan barked, firing again.

The creature shrieked, its form writhing and distorting. The light from their flashlights flickered and died, plunging the house into darkness. The growls grew louder, echoing from every direction.

Morgan grabbed Carla's arm, pulling her toward the stairs. "We need to get out of here. Now!"

They raced down the stairs, the creature's tendrils slamming into the walls behind them. The house groaned as if under immense pressure, and the air felt like it was being sucked away.

Bursting out the front door, they sprinted to the cruiser. Morgan fumbled with the keys, his hands shaking as he started the engine. The headlights illuminated the farmhouse, where the creature loomed in the doorway, its many faces twisted in rage.

As they sped away, the growls faded, but the chill in the air remained.

Back at the sheriff's office, Morgan and Carla sat in silence, their breaths ragged. Emily's journal lay open on the desk, her final warning staring back at them.

"It was never truly gone."

Carla broke the silence. "What do we do now?"

Morgan leaned forward, his eyes hard. "We find a way to finish this. For good."

The faint hum of the lights flickered, casting long shadows across the room. In the corner, for just a moment, the darkness seemed to shift.

The Shadow Eater was still out there, and the battle was far from over.

<u>Message from the Author:</u>

I hope you enjoyed this book, I love astrology and knew there was not a book such as this out on the shelf. I love metaphysical items as well. Please check out my other books:

-Life of Government Benefits

-My life of Hell

-My life with Hydrocephalus

-Red Sky

-World Domination:Woman's rule

-World Domination:Woman's Rule 2: The War

-Life and Banishment of Apophis: book 1

-The Kidney Friendly Diet

-The Ultimate Hemp Cookbook

-Creating a Dispensary(legally)

-Cleanliness throughout life: the importance of showering from childhood to adulthood.

-Strong Roots: The Risks of Overcoddling children

-Hemp Horoscopes: Cosmic Insights and Earthly Healing

- Celestial Hemp Navigating the Zodiac: Through the Green Cosmos

-Astrological Hemp: Aligning The Stars with Earth's Ancient Herb

-The Astrological Guide to Hemp: Stars, Signs, and Sacred Leaves

-Green Growth: Innovative Marketing Strategies for your Hemp Products and Dispensary

-Cosmic Cannabis
-Astrological Munchies
-Henry The Hemp
-Zodiacal Roots: The Astrological Soul Of Hemp
- Green Constellations: Intersection of Hemp and Zodiac
-Hemp in The Houses: An astrological Adventure Through The Cannabis Galaxy
-Galactic Ganja Guide
Heavenly Hemp
Zodiac Leaves
Doctor Who Astrology
Cannastrology
Stellar Satvias and Cosmic Indicas
<u>Celestial Cannabis: A Zodiac Journey</u>
AstroHerbology: The Sky and The Soil: Volume 1
AstroHerbology:Celestial Cannabis:Volume 2
Cosmic Cannabis Cultivation
The Starry Guide to Herbal Harmony: Volume 1
The Starry Guide to Herbal Harmony: Cannabis Universe: Volume 2
Yugioh Astrology: Astrological Guide to Deck, Duels and more
Nightmare Mansion: Echoes of The Abyss
Nightmare Mansion 2: Legacy of Shadows
Nightmare Mansion 3: Shadows of the Forgotten
Nightmare Mansion 4: Echoes of the Damned
The Life and Banishment of Apophis: Book 2
Nightmare Mansion: Halls of Despair
<u>Healing with Herb: Cannabis and Hydrocephalus</u>
<u>Planetary Pot: Aligning with Astrological Herbs: Volume 1</u>
Fast Track to Freedom: 30 Days to Financial Independence Using AI, Assets, and Agile Hustles
<u>Cosmic Hemp Pathways</u>

How to Become Financially Free in 30 Days: 10,000 Paths to Prosperity
Zodiacal Herbage: Astrological Insights: Volume 1
Nightmare Mansion: Whispers in the Walls
The Daleks Invade Atlantis
Henry the hemp and Hydrocephalus

10X The Kidney Friendly Diet
Cannabis Universe: Adult coloring book
Hemp Astrology: The Healing Power of the Stars
Zodiacal Herbage: Astrological Insights: Cannabis Universe: Volume 2
Planetary Pot: Aligning with Astrological Herbs: Cannabis Universes: Volume 2
Doctor Who Meets the Replicators and SG-1: The Ultimate Battle for Survival
Nightmare Mansion: Curse of the Blood Moon
The Celestial Stoner: A Guide to the Zodiac
Cosmic Pleasures: Sex Toy Astrology for Every Sign
Hydrocephalus Astrology: Navigating the Stars and Healing Waters
Lapis and the Mischievous Chocolate Bar

Celestial Positions: Sexual Astrology for Every Sign
Apophis's Shadow Work Journal: : A Journey of Self-Discovery and Healing
Kinky Cosmos: Sexual Kink Astrology for Every Sign
Digital Cosmos: The Astrological Digimon Compendium
Stellar Seeds: The Cosmic Guide to Growing with Astrology
Apophis's Daily Gratitude Journal

Cat Astrology: Feline Mysteries of the Cosmos
The Cosmic Kama Sutra: An Astrological Guide to Sexual Positions

Unleash Your Potential: A Guided Journal Powered by AI Insights

Whispers of the Enchanted Grove

Cosmic Pleasures: An Astrological Guide to Sexual Kinks

369, 12 Manifestation Journal

Whisper of the nocturne journal(blank journal for writing or drawing)

The Boogey Book

Locked In Reflection: A Chastity Journey Through Locktober

Generating Wealth Quickly:

How to Generate $100,000 in 24 Hours

Star Magic: Harness the Power of the Universe

The Flatulence Chronicles: A Fart Journal for Self-Discovery

The Doctor and The Death Moth

Seize the Day: A Personal Seizure Tracking Journal

The Ultimate Boogeyman Safari: A Journey into the Boogie World and Beyond

Whispers of Samhain: 1,000 Spells of Love, Luck, and Lunar Magic: Samhain Spell Book

Apophis's guides:

Witch's Spellbook Crafting Guide for Halloween

<u>**Frost & Flame: The Enchanted Yule Grimoire of 1000 Winter Spells**</u>

<u>**The Ultimate Boogey Goo Guide & Spooky Activities for Halloween Fun**</u>

Harmony of the Scales: A Libra's Spellcraft for Balance and Beauty

The Enchanted Advent: 36 Days of Christmas Wonders

Nightmare Mansion: The Labyrinth of Screams

Harvest of Enchantment: 1,000 Spells of Gratitude, Love, and Fortune for Thanksgiving

The Boogey Chronicles: A Journal of Nightly Encounters and Shadowy Secrets

The 12 Days of Financial Freedom: A Step-by-Step Christmas Countdown to Transform Your Finances

Sigil of the Eternal Spiral Blank Journal

A Christmas Feast: Timeless Recipes for Every Meal

Holiday Stress-Free Solutions: A Survival Guide to Thriving During the Festive Season

Yu-Gi-Oh! Holiday Gifting Mastery: The Ultimate Guide for Fans and Newcomers Alike

Holiday Harmony: A Hydrocephalus Survival Guide for the Festive Season

Celestial Craft: The Witch's Almanac for 2025 – A Cosmic Guide to Manifestations, Moons, and Mystical Events

Doctor Who: The Toymaker's Winter Wonderland

Tulsa King Unveiled: A Thrilling Guide to Stallone's Mafia Masterpiece

Pendulum Craft: A Complete Guide to Crafting and Using Personalized Divination Tools

Nightmare Mansion: Santa's Eternal Eve

Starlight Noel: A Cosmic Journey through Christmas Mysteries

The Dark Architect: Unlocking the Blueprint of Existence

Surviving the Embrace: The Ultimate Guide to Encounters with The Hugging Molly

The Enchanted Codex: Secrets of the Craft for Witches, Wiccans, and Pagans

Harvest of Gratitude: A Complete Thanksgiving Guide

Yuletide Essentials: A Complete Guide to an Authentic and Magical Christmas

Celestial Smokes: A Cosmic Guide to Cigars and Astrology

Living in Balance: A Comprehensive Survival Guide to Thriving with Diabetes Insipidus

Cosmic Symbiosis: The Venom Zodiac Chronicles

The Cursed Paw of Ambition

Cosmic Symbiosis: The Astrological Venom Journal

Celestial Wonders Unfold: A Stargazer's Guide to the Cosmos (2024-2029)

The Ultimate Black Friday Prepper's Guide: Mastering Shopping Strategies and Savings

Cosmic Sales: The Astrological Guide to Black Friday Shopping

Legends of the Corn Mother and Other Harvest Myths

Whispers of the Harvest: The Corn Mother's Journal

The Evergreen Spellbook

The Doctor Meets the Boogeyman

The White Witch of Rose Hall's SpellBook

The Gingerbread Golem's Shadow: A Study in Sweet Darkness

The Gingerbread Golem Codex: An Academic Exploration of Sweet Myths

The Gingerbread Golem Grimoire: Sweet Magicks and Spells for the Festive Witch

The Curse of the Gingerbread Golem

10-minute Christmas Crafts for kids

<u>Christmas Crisis Solutions: The Ultimate Last-Minute Survival Guide</u>

Gingerbread Golem Recipes: Holiday Treats with a Magical Twist

The Infinite Key: Unlocking Mystical Secrets of the Ages

Enchanted Yule: A Wiccan and Pagan Guide to a Magical and Memorable Season

Dinosaurs of Power: Unlocking Ancient Magick

Astro-Dinos: The Cosmic Guide to Prehistoric Wisdom

Gallifrey's Yule Logs: A Festive Doctor Who Cookbook

The Dino Grimoire: Secrets of Prehistoric Magick

The Gift They Never Knew They Needed

The Gingerbread Golem's Culinary Alchemy: Enchanting Recipes for a Sweetly Dark Feast

A Time Lord Christmas: Holiday Adventures with the Doctor

Krampusproofing Your Home: Defensive Strategies for Yule

Silent Frights: A Collection of Christmas Creepypastas to Chill Your Bones

Santa Raptor's Jolly Carnage: A Dino-Claus Christmas Tale

Prehistoric Palettes: A Dino Wicca Coloring Journey

The Christmas Wishkeeper Chronicles

The Starlight Sleigh: A Holiday Journey

Elf Secrets: The True Magic of the North Pole

Candy Cane Conjurations

Cooking with Kids: Recipes Under 20 Minutes

Doctor Who: The TARDIS Confiscation

The Anxiety First Aid Kit: Quick Tools to Calm Your Mind

Frosty Whispers: A Winter's Tale

The Infinite Key: Unlocking the Secrets to Prosperity, Resilience, and Purpose

The Grasping Void: Why You'll Regret This Purchase

Astrology for Busy Bees: Star Signs Simplified

The Instant Focus Formula: Cut Through the Noise

The Secret Language of Colors: Unlocking the Emotional Codes

Sacred Fossil Chronicles: Blank Journal

The Christmas Cottage Miracle

Feeding Frenzy: Graboid-Inspired Recipes

Manifest in Minutes: The Quick Law of Attraction Guide

The Symbiote Chronicles: Doctor Who's Venomous Journey

Think Tiny, Grow Big: The Minimalist Mindset

The Energy Key: Unlocking Limitless Motivation

New Year, New Magic: Manifesting Your Best Year Yet

Unstoppable You: Mastering Confidence in Minutes

Infinite Energy: The Secret to Never Feeling Drained

Lightning Focus: Mastering the Art of Productivity in a Distracted World

Saturnalia Manifestation Magick: A Guide to Unlocking Abundance During the Solstice

Graboids and Garland: The Ultimate Tremors-Themed Christmas Guide

12 Nights of Holiday Magic

The Power of Pause: 60-Second Mindfulness Practices

The Quick Reset: How to Reclaim Your Life After Burnout

If you want solar for your home go here: https://www.harborsolar.live/apophisenterprises/

Get Some Tarot cards: https://www.makeplayingcards.com/sell/apophis-occult-shop

<u>**Get   some   shirts: https://www.bonfire.com/store/apophis-shirt-emporium/**</u>

Instagrams:
@apophis_enterprises,
@apophisbookemporium,
@apophisscardshop
Twitter: @apophisenterpr1
Tiktok:@apophisenterprise
Youtube: @sg1fan23477, @FiresideRetreatKingdom
Hive: @sg1fan23477
CheeLee: @SG1fan23477

Podcast: Apophis Chat Zone: https://open.spotify.com/show/
5zXbrCLEV2xzCp8ybrfHsk?si=fb4d4fdbdce44dec

Newsletter: https://apophiss-newsletter-27c897.beehiiv.com/

If you want to support me or see posts of other projects that I have come over to: **buymeacoffee.com/mpetchinskg**

I post there daily several times a day

Get your Dinowicca or Christmas themed digital products, especially Santa Raptor songs and other musics. Here:
https://sg1fan23477.gumroad.com

Apophis Yuletide Digital has not only digital Christmas items, but it will have all things with Dinowicca as well as other Digital products.